Tl
pu
with donations
made to the
GiveBIG
for Books
Campaign.

Showdown at the
Alamo

CATCH ALL OF FLAT STANLEY'S WORLDWIDE ADVENTURES:

AND DON'T MISS ANY OF THESE OUTRAGEOUS STORIES:

FLAT STANLEY's WORLDWIDE ADVENTURES (10)

BOOK No.

Showdown at the Alamo

CREATED BY **Jeff Brown**
WRITTEN BY **Josh Greenhut**
PICTURES BY **Macky Pamintuan**

HARPER
An Imprint of HarperCollinsPublishers

Flat Stanley's Worldwide Adventures #10: Showdown at the Alamo
Text copyright © 2014 by the Trust u/w/o Richard C. Brown a/k/a Jeff Brown f/b/o Duncan Brown.
Illustrations by Macky Pamintuan, copyright © 2014 by HarperCollins Publishers.

Library of Congress Cataloging-in-Publication Data
Greenhut, Josh.
    Showdown at the Alamo / created by Jeff Brown ; written by Josh Greenhut ; pictures by Macky Pamintuan. — First edition.
        pages   cm. — (Flat Stanley's worldwide adventures ; #10)
    Summary: Autograph-seekers interfere with Stanley Lambchop's hopes for a fun vacation with friends while sightseeing in Texas.
    ISBN 978-0-06-218988-2 (trade bdg.) — ISBN 978-0-06-218987-5 (pbk.)
    [1. Vacations—Fiction. 2. Celebrities—Fiction. 3. Friendship—Fiction. 4. Alamo (San Antonio, Tex.)—Fiction. 5. Texas—Fiction.] I. Pamintuan, Macky, illustrator. II. Brown, Jeff, 1926–2003. III. Title.
PZ7.G84568Sho 2014   2013021853
[Fic]—dc23   CIP
                                                                        AC

Typography by Alison Klapthor
13 14 15 16 17   CG/RRDC   10 9 8 7 6 5 4 3 2 1
❖
First Edition

CONTENTS

A Rattlesnake in a Hurricane

"Look—we're entering Texas!" cried Stanley's mother, Harriett Lambchop, as she sped down the highway. From the backseat Stanley could see an oncoming sign welcoming them to the Lone Star State.

"It's so flat!" said Stanley, looking out at the plains.

"You should know," teased Stanley's

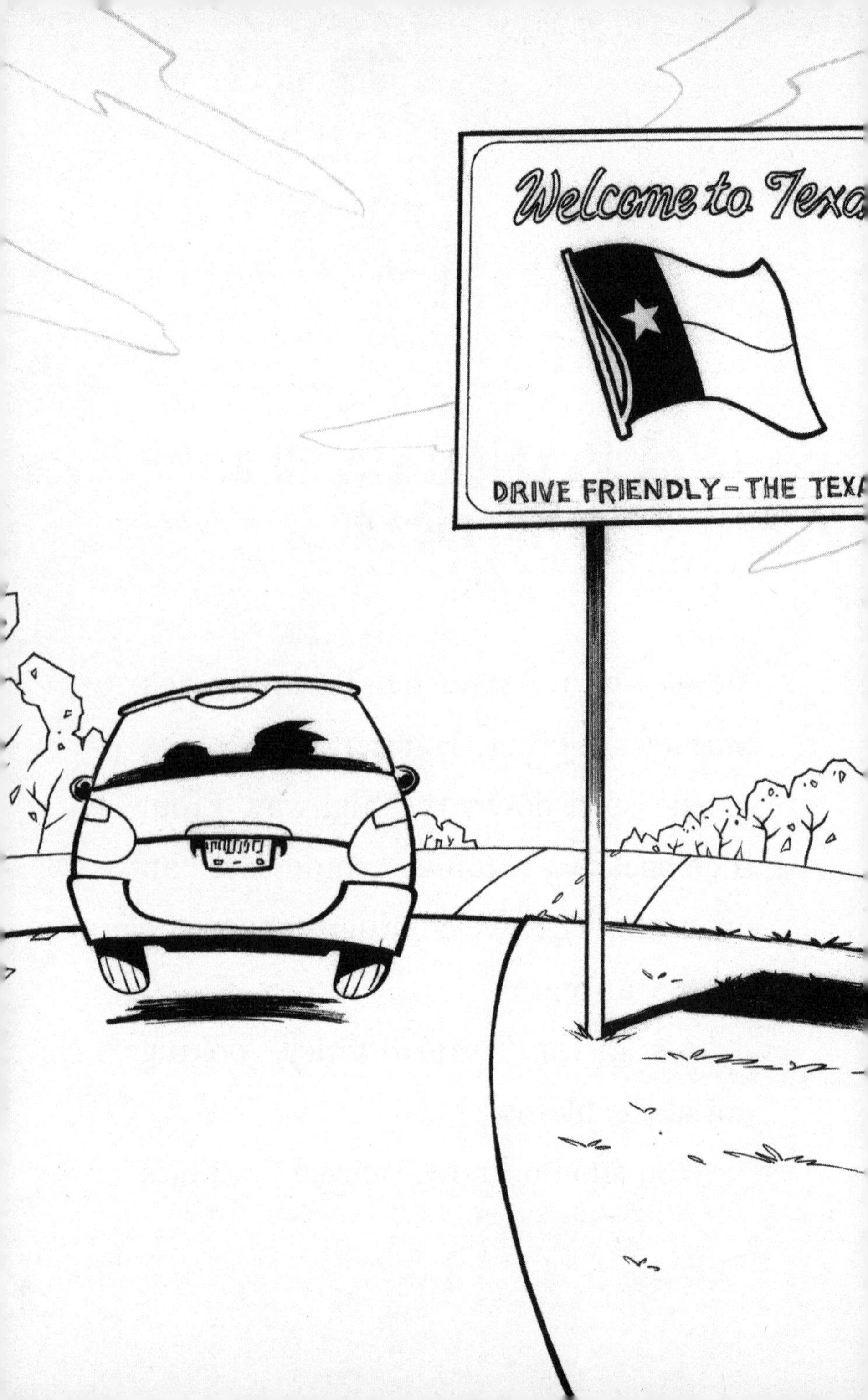

Welcome to Texa
DRIVE FRIENDLY - THE TEXA

brother, Arthur. On the other side of Arthur sat their friend Carlos, who was studying a map.

"Of course it's flat, amigo," said Carlos. "Look at this." He handed the map over, and Stanley spread it on his lap.

Ever since the bulletin board over his bed had fallen and flattened him, Stanley had been only half an inch thick. That made his lap an especially good travel table.

"Do you see how that rectangular section near the top looks like a handle you could pick up the whole state with?" asked Carlos. "We're in the Texas panhandle!"

"How long until we get to Austin?" Arthur asked. The boys were going there to visit Carlos's cousin Eduardo. Stanley had been looking forward to it for weeks!

"Only nine more hours," Mrs. Lambchop replied from behind the wheel.

Texas is a very big state, thought Stanley.

Stanley loved maps. Since being flattened, he had traveled all over the world, often by mail. He had been to Japan, Australia, Kenya, China, and Egypt. Mexico was where he had met Carlos's cousin Eduardo, who was now a student at the University of Texas at Austin.

Stanley followed along on the map as they drove. Amarillo was in the center of the panhandle. Outside the city, they passed a woman on a horse herding cattle. She was wearing a cowboy hat, and Stanley thought of his old friend Calamity Jasper, who he and Arthur had met on a family trip to Mount Rushmore. She'd ridden with Stanley rolled up on the back of her horse.

If we drove north in a straight line, Stanley realized, we would hit South Dakota, where Calamity lives!

"Look, boys, it's the real Cadillac Ranch!" announced his mother.

Stanley looked up to see ten brightly painted cars sticking out of the ground along the highway, like half-buried dominoes.

"Cadillac Ranch is an art display that was created in the seventies," Mrs. Lambchop explained.

"Cool!" Arthur said, reaching over

and opening the window as they drove by for a better look.

Air rushed in, and the map on Stanley's lap fluttered out the open window. He leaned out to catch it.

The wind slammed into Stanley, catching his upper body like a sail.

Oh no! Before Stanley knew what was happening, he had been pulled through the window and out of the car. In an instant the only thing keeping him down was his feet, which he had managed to hook around his seat belt.

"Aaaaaahhhhhh!!" he screamed in terror as the car barreled down the highway. His body flapped out the window like a scarf.

"STANLEY!" his mother shrieked. The car swerved wildly.

"Hold on!" Carlos yelled as he and Arthur tried to pull him back in.

Suddenly there was a siren and

red-and-blue flashing lights. A police officer on a motorcycle pulled alongside their car. With a concerned look at Stanley, he motioned for Mrs. Lambchop to pull over to the side of the road.

The policeman got off his motorcycle and asked them all to step out of the car. He stood in front of Stanley and took off his sunglasses. "Lil' feller, just what were you doin' flyin' out the window at eighty-five miles an hour like a rattlesnake in a hurricane?"

Stanley couldn't stop shaking like a leaf. Getting sucked out the window had been very frightening. And now I'm in trouble with the law! he thought.

"Armadillo got your tongue?" the officer said.

"It wasn't Stanley's fault," Carlos blurted.

"Stanley gets caught in the wind," agreed Arthur. "He's been blown clear

across Canada *and* Australia!"

The officer nodded slowly, then he said, "Any o' you fellers know what the word *Texas* means?"

Mrs. Lambchop's hand shot into the air. She waved it wildly like an excited student in class. Stanley knew how much his mother loved language trivia of any kind.

"Ma'am?"

"It's the Caddo Indian word for 'friends'!"

"Right as a rutabaga root, ma'am," the officer said, impressed.

"I'm the social representative for the Grammar Society," Mrs. Lambchop said with pride. "I'm attending the Texas

Librarians' Convention this weekend!"

"Well, you're not the only one who knows your buts from your bees," said the officer. "Judgin' from how these boys stuck up for their flat friend here, I'd say they know the meaning of Texas just fine." The officer leaned in toward Stanley. "Just try and keep the flapjack in the frying pan next time, all right?"

"Yes, sir," Stanley said with relief.

"One more thing," the officer said. He pulled out a pen and pad of paper, and Stanley thought he was going to write them a ticket. Instead the officer held both items out to Stanley.

"My grandmammy's more stuck on you than tumbleweed on a cactus! Can

I have your autograph? She'll never believe in a million years that I pulled over Flat Stanley Lambchop!"

Rockin' the Texas Capital

Stanley was so excited to see Eduardo again, he almost wished they hadn't needed to stop for the night. When they arrived at the University of Texas the next morning, he, Arthur, and Carlos couldn't wait to get out of the car.

The plan was for the boys to stay with Eduardo while Stanley's mother attended the Texas Librarians'

Convention in San Antonio, which was less than a couple of hours away.

The four of them waited for Eduardo in front of the clock tower in the center of campus. Not long ago Eduardo had guided Stanley on a trek through Mexico, giving long lectures about the country's history as they went. Stanley could still hear Eduardo's voice describing the achievements of the ancient Mayans. Now Eduardo was a college student studying history!

"There he is!" said Carlos, bolting across the giant courtyard to meet his older cousin.

Eduardo came over and patted Stanley on the back. "My amigo, you

are even flatter than I remember you being!"

"You got taller!" said Stanley.

A moment later they all were following Eduardo to his dorm on the edge of campus. It was the first time Stanley had ever been to a university. Students strode back and forth along the paved pathways, clutching their bags and books. A line of burly men in football jerseys jogged by. Eduardo cried, "GO LONGHORNS!" and held up a fist with his forefinger and pinky finger raised like the horns of a bull. After the players had passed, he said, "Texas is a place where everything is big, but football may be biggest of all."

After the boys had dropped their bags off at Eduardo's dorm room, it was time for Stanley's mother to go.

"Boys, I want you to have a good time," she said. "Eduardo, you're in charge, and I'm trusting you to be responsible. I want all of you to promise me three things. One: Drive safely."

Eduardo nodded. "You have my word, Mrs. Lambchop."

"Two: You will meet me at the Alamo in San Antonio at noon the day after tomorrow."

Arthur checked his watch.

"Three: Follow these rules at all times." Mrs. Lambchop held up a book.

"*The Rules of English Grammar*?" read Carlos.

Mrs. Lambchop nodded and handed him the book. She was very serious about the proper use of language. "Now I must be on my way to the Texas Librarians' Convention."

Mrs. Lambchop kissed Stanley twice—once on the forehead and once on the backhead—hugged Arthur, and left.

The boys looked at one another excitedly. Eduardo rubbed his hands together. "Let the fun begin, amigos!"

He led them away from the dorm and back toward the center of campus. "Who knows what Austin is the capital of?"

"Texas?" guessed Arthur, rushing to keep up.

"That is true," said Eduardo. "What else?"

"Football?" guessed Stanley.

"That is also true in my opinion," said Eduardo. "But what else?"

No one answered.

They came to a big grassy field, which was filled with people sitting on blankets gathered in front of a stage. "Well, amigos," said Eduardo, "you are about to find out!"

The boys followed him to the front near the stage. He motioned for them to stay put.

Suddenly the crowd started cheering as a band of musicians took their places.

"Where is Eduardo going?" Arthur asked. But then Stanley saw that Eduardo had joined the band and picked up a guitar.

"Welcome to the music festival!" Eduardo yelled into his microphone. "Now what is Austin the capital of?!"

"Live music!" the crowd shouted back.

"What?" Eduardo put one hand up to his ear and with the other he pointed to Stanley and the boys in the front row. "My friends down here can't hear you!"

"LIVE MUSIC!"

With a yowl, Eduardo chopped at his guitar, and sound flooded the air. Stanley had never heard such loud music before. With every beat, his whole body vibrated as if he were the skin of a drum. It was like the music was coming from inside him.

When the song ended, Eduardo grinned at the three of them, sweat streaming down his face. "This next song is for a good friend," he said into the microphone. "I hope you like it." The drummer counted off, and Eduardo sang:

"My amigo Stanley,
he's so flat!

Like he fell from the sky
and his body went splat!

"He travels round the world
to show us where it's at.
Man, he's smooth
as a flat butter pat!

"Show your gratitude!
Get the flattitude!
Stay true to yourself
and you'll never fall flat!

"Show your gratitude!
Get the flattitude!
Rock like the kid
who rolls like a mat!"

Eduardo leaned down and pulled Stanley up on the stage. The crowd went wild when they saw Stanley. Eduardo bent him so his back was arched and his hands and feet were on the ground. The drummer tossed Eduardo a pair of drumsticks, and he started tapping Stanley's stomach and chest.

With each beat of the drumsticks, Stanley's body made a hollow *thwop*! It sounded like when Arthur opened his mouth wide and flicked his cheek with his finger.

As Eduardo played him, Stanley struggled not to giggle, because it tickled. Once he relaxed, he felt the beat of his body meld with the vibrations

from the bass drum. He tapped his feet.
He couldn't stop smiling.

When Eduardo finished his solo,

Stanley leaped up, and he, the band, and the crowd all shouted the last chorus together.

> "Show your gratitude!
> Get the flattitude!
> Rock like the kid
> who rolls like a mat!"

Driven Underground

When the song ended with a cymbal crash, Stanley was overwhelmed by all the people screaming his name. Someone leaped onto the stage and tried to hug him, but Stanley slid out from under her arms. Suddenly the crowd rushed the stage like a tidal wave. The microphone stand was knocked to the ground, and Stanley lost his balance.

What if I get trampled? he thought. He tucked his head to his chest and rolled himself up. Then he heard Arthur's muffled voice: "We have to get Stanley out of here!"

"Eduardo, you're the strongest!" said Carlos.

"Hold on, Stanley!" hollered Eduardo. He lifted Stanley up and tossed him off the stage like a giant bowling ball. Stanley's body barreled through the crowd, his head spinning. He could hear people jumping out of his way. He rolled on, his friends close behind.

The mob of fans did not stop chasing them until they were halfway across campus.

An hour later Eduardo peeked out
from between the curtains of his dorm

room, watching the crowd of people outside. "I cannot believe it," he said. "They're still there. There's even one girl in a cowboy hat who looks really dangerous." More than a dozen fans had occupied the sidewalk outside Eduardo's dorm. Every once in a while Stanley could hear them chanting his name.

Stanley was draped over the back of the couch. His stomach grumbled. Eduardo had ordered pizza, but it hadn't arrived yet.

Carlos said, "Does this always happen when you travel, Stanley?"

Stanley didn't answer.

"It's gotten worse since he won the

National Medal of Achievement on TV," Arthur said.

"I wish I had this many girls chasing me," said Eduardo with admiration.

Stanley grimaced.

Carlos said, "On the way here, Señora Lambchop got pulled over by the police, and instead of giving us a ticket, the officer just asked Stanley for his autograph!"

There was a knock on the door. Eduardo walked over to look through the peephole. "Pizza!" he called.

While Eduardo paid the driver, Stanley carried the pizza over to the coffee table and opened the box.

Staring up at him was a fan letter

resting right on top of the pizza. In flowery letters someone had written the words COME OUTSIDE, STANLEY!

With a grunt, Stanley tore the note in half.

"What's wrong, amigo?" Carlos said.

"I just want to hang out with my friends this weekend!" Stanley said. "In peace and quiet!"

"I know what we should do," Eduardo announced after a moment. "Go camping! Get away from all this loco attention."

"Are we allowed?" Carlos asked.

"I don't think our mom would mind," said Arthur, "as long as we drive safely, show up at the Alamo on time, and use good grammar."

"I have a car and camping gear," said Eduardo. "I even know a dude ranch where we can get horses. We'll go riding and camping, just the four of us, and then I'll take you to meet your mother in San Antonio."

The boys scarfed down their pizza and packed up their things. Since they were on the ground floor, they snuck out the back window. Stanley went first, and the others slid down his body. They crept to Eduardo's car and piled in. The car peeled away, and the shouts of Stanley's fans quickly faded into the distance.

There's nothing better, thought Stanley, than four guys together on the open road!

Flying High

Stanley was impressed by how carefully Eduardo drove, obeying Stanley's mother's first rule. They left the city and were soon in a red landscape of cacti and low bushes.

Eventually they came to a small town. There was a main street lined with low buildings that looked like part of a set from one of the old western movies Stanley's father loved. They passed a saloon and an old-fashioned-looking bank. Eduardo parked in front of a building with a sign that read BIG BILL'S DUDE RANCH.

A man with a gray handlebar mustache and a ten-gallon hat lumbered down the dusty porch and waved to them. "Welcome to Bandera, the cowboy capital of the whole doggone world! The name's Big Bill. You bandits fixin' to saddle up?"

"Yes, sir!" said Carlos.

"We need two horses to ride into the wilderness for an overnight camping trip," said Eduardo.

"I have just the horses for you," said

Big Bill. He led Stanley, Carlos, and Eduardo toward a stable to the side of the building.

"Hey!" said Arthur.

"Hay is for horses, Arthur," said Stanley. Their mother was always correcting Arthur when he said that. "Don't forget your grammar."

"That's what I meant!" said Arthur, pointing to a bale of hay beside a hitching post. "It's hay!"

"This here is Sam Houston," Big Bill said, patting a brown horse with a white star on its nose. "Named after the first elected president of the Republic of Texas. Y'all know that before it was a state, Texas was its own country for a while? Real independent. Sam Houston here has a mind of his own." Stanley laid his hand against the side of the horse, and Sam Houston gave a friendly shudder.

The man moved over and tightened the saddle on a black horse. "And this is Davy Crockett. You heard o' him? The King of the Wild Frontier? He fought at the Alamo. Bet you didn't know that the real Davy Crockett was a congressman from Tennessee." He patted the horse. "Anyway, Davy here used to have a coonskin cap, but he ate it."

Stanley grinned. "Thanks, Big Bill," he said.

Their saddlebags were packed with supplies for the night, and Carlos and Eduardo rode together on Sam Houston, while Arthur and Stanley rode Davy Crockett. Stanley had not ridden a horse since their friend Calamity Jasper had taken him and Arthur looking for gold in South Dakota. He'd forgotten how

fun and bouncy it was.

With Sam Houston and Davy Crockett kicking up clouds of dust behind them, Stanley and his fellow cowboys rode into the Texan wilderness.

Stanley's flat legs were just starting to hurt from slapping against the sides of his horse when Arthur suggested they stop to drink from their canteens. As Stanley dismounted, the wind picked up. He held on to Davy Crockett's reins as the wind blew him a few feet off the ground.

"It's getting windy," Stanley said nervously.

Arthur poked a finger in the air. "Good kite weather!" he announced. Since Stanley had been flattened, Arthur often enjoyed flying him on a string on weekends.

"How about parasailing?" said Carlos.

Stanley's mouth went dry.

"Come on, Stanley," said Arthur. "It'll be fun."

Stanley swallowed. The wind scared him—especially since it had dragged him out the car window—but he didn't want to let his friends down.

"Okay," he croaked.

Eduardo dug a rope out of one of the bags. Carlos tied one end to Sam

Houston's saddle and the other end around Stanley.

"Ready?" Eduardo called from atop Sam Houston.

With a grunt, Carlos lifted Stanley up over his head like a board, and they grabbed each other's wrists.

"Whatever you do, don't let go," Stanley said.

"Whatever you do, don't drop me," Carlos replied with a chuckle.

"Ready!" they shouted together.

"Hi-ya!" Eduardo kicked Sam Houston into a gallop. Carlos jumped up as the rope went taut. Stanley shut his eyes tight, and they were airborne.

The air current lifted Stanley's chest,

and he pulled Carlos up with him. The boys floated higher and higher, until they were almost directly above Eduardo's and Arthur's galloping horses.

Carlos let out a high-pitched "yi, yi, yi, yi, yi!"

"I'm next!" cried Arthur from below.

This is fun, Stanley realized. He opened his eyes, and the view took his breath away. "It's beautiful!" he called from his place high in the air.

The sky and the land both seemed bigger than they were at home. To one side there were rolling green hills spreading as far as Stanley could see. To the other, Stanley spied an endless expanse of prairies. The dimmest outline of mountains was on the horizon.

Stanley had learned in school that Texas was the second-biggest state after Alaska. It sure looks that big from up here, thought Stanley.

Carlos pulled one of Stanley's hands, and Stanley banked to the right. Carlos pulled the other, and they swooped left. He pulled both and they dived.

"Yee-haw!" cried Stanley, swooping up again.

Suddenly Stanley saw a flash of black out of the corner of his eye.

"BIRDS!" Carlos screamed.

They flew through the flock as if

it were a black cloud. Dodging a bird,
Carlos loosened his grip.

"Carlos!" screamed Stanley. He bent
his fingers, catching Carlos's hand.
Stanley's left side dipped, trying to

hold his friend. The ground rushed up. "We're going to crash!" yelled Carlos.

"HELP!" Stanley cried.

Amid a thundering of hooves, a hand reached out. "I have you!" Stanley's brother called. He pulled Carlos onto the back of Davy Crockett, and Stanley floated down onto the horse's rump behind them.

"You saved us, amigo," Carlos said breathlessly to Arthur.

Stanley reached over and squeezed his brother's shoulder in gratitude.

"I think that's enough excitement for today!" Eduardo announced from alongside them. "Let's find a place to camp!"

On the Run

The boys tied their horses to a tree near a low stone hill called Enchanted Rock.

As they had collected firewood, Enchanted Rock had glowed a bright, fiery pink in the setting sun. Now the rock lurked in the dark behind their campsite. Stanley's stomach growled as he fanned the glowing embers of the campfire with his arm.

"Some Native American tribes believe Enchanted Rock is a doorway to the spirit world," Eduardo said.

The light from the fire flickered on Eduardo's face. Suddenly a strange, otherworldly moaning rose up all around them, as if from the center of the earth. "What's that?" Arthur shrieked, lifting Stanley up and hiding behind him.

Eduardo laughed. "The Tonkawa tribe says it is ghosts. Scientists say it is just the sound of the rock cooling after being heated by the sun all day."

"Put me down, Arthur," Stanley grumbled as he was placed on the ground.

Stanley grabbed a can of beans from his pack, pulled open the top, and put the can on the fire. "Calamity Jasper says a cowboy always travels with a can of beans," he said.

"Calamity Jasper? Who's that?" Eduardo wondered aloud.

"We met her a while back in the Black Hills of South Dakota," said Arthur. "I singlehandedly saved her life when she was trapped in a gold mine."

"You did not," Stanley said, rolling his eyes. "But she did teach us to build a campfire." Stanley smiled, thinking about her. "She's a good friend," he said simply.

Stanley and the other boys talked late

into the night . . . about bullfighting in Mexico, how many tacos they could eat in one sitting, whether there was life on other planets, and their biggest fears.

Stanley stoked the glowing coals of the fire with a stick. "There's a part of me that's getting scared to go outside on a windy day. I keep getting blown away."

His friends nodded in understanding. Somehow that was all it took to make Stanley feel better.

At last Arthur draped Stanley over him for warmth, and Stanley pulled a blanket over them both.

"Good night, guys," Stanley said with a yawn.

The boys murmured their soft replies
and drifted off to sleep.

* * *

Early the next morning the boys ate some dry cereal and packed up camp. Stanley wished they could stay another night, but they had to be at the Alamo by noon. Arthur set the alarm on his watch to make sure they wouldn't be late.

Riding back to Bandera, they galloped over rocks and between cacti. They skirted a red canyon. The sun rose higher and higher.

In a few hours Big Bill's Dude Ranch appeared in the distance. As they got closer, Stanley could see a group of people gathered around the porch. They were less than a hundred yards away when Stanley read a sign a girl was holding: I'M FLAT-OUT IN LOVE! His stomach sank as he realized it was a group of fans looking for him.

The boys pulled Sam Houston and Davy Crockett to a stop.

"Looks like Stanleymania has caught up with us," said Arthur.

"What should we do?" asked Carlos.

"I have an idea," Eduardo said. "Stanley, do you still have that map of Texas?"

Stanley nodded.

Eduardo jumped down from his horse and rummaged through his saddlebag. He pulled out a Magic Marker. "We're going to smuggle you out of here."

To stay out of sight, Stanley lay draped facedown over Davy Crockett like a blanket. As Carlos and Eduardo tied up the horses, Stanley could hear Big Bill answering questions on the porch of the dude ranch. "Yes, ma'am!" he said. "That does sound like him! About this high"—he held his hand up to his belly—"and this thick." He pinched his fingers together.

Eduardo slipped Stanley his disguise: It was the sign he had written on the back of the map. In big letters it read WHOM DO WE WANT? STANLEY! The boys had argued about whether it should say "who" or "whom." Finally they checked Mrs. Lambchop's book of grammar rules. To Stanley's surprise, "whom" was correct.

Stanley jumped down from the horse and held the sign in front of his face. Eduardo lifted him up. Stanley kept his thin side out, and Eduardo walked calmly to the car, looking as if he were just another Stanley fan toting a sign.

The boys jumped in the car with their things, and Eduardo hit the gas. Just when Stanley thought the coast was clear, Arthur cried, "We've got company!" A big pickup truck had pulled out of the parking lot after them.

We're being chased! Stanley realized.

"Your fans really are loco about you," said Carlos in disbelief. The truck was visible in their rearview mirror.

"Lucky me," Stanley huffed.

"Maybe you'll get kidnapped!"

Arthur said excitedly. He started telling Carlos and Eduardo about what happened when they mailed Stanley to Oda Nobu, the martial arts star in Japan. Some fans had kidnapped Oda Nobu and Stanley, and Arthur had had to rescue them.

"Being famous isn't as fun as it's cracked up to be," said Stanley when Arthur was finished.

"One of our cousins, the great matador Carmen del Junco, says that being famous is a responsibility," said Carlos.

"Hmph," grumbled Stanley. "I don't need more responsibility. I don't even like to clean my room."

"Come on," said Arthur. "It's not that bad. Everybody *loves* you."

Stanley frowned.

"You get to do whatever you want!" Arthur continued.

"I just want to be treated like a normal kid," argued Stanley. "I want to hang out with my friends and play outside and get in trouble without it ending up in the newspaper." He glanced back at the truck chasing them. "They think I'm some kind of idol. But I'm not. I'm just like them. It's just that I'm . . . flatter."

"Then it is true what they say," said Eduardo. "Flattery will get you nowhere."

Even Stanley couldn't help laughing at that. Eduardo turned onto a side road, but the truck swerved and kept following them.

"What's that up ahead?" Stanley asked. In the distance, a field of giant white windmills, as tall as apartment buildings, rose into view.

"It's a wind farm," said Eduardo. "Texas is home to some of the biggest wind farms in the world. They can be hundreds of miles wide."

Stanley's chest tightened. His sides curled slightly.

"Turn around!" he croaked.

"What's wrong?" asked Eduardo.

"They're right behind us," said Carlos.

"TURN AROUND!" Stanley repeated, his whole body shaking.

"But, Stanley—" Arthur began.

"No, Arthur!" cried Stanley. "Remember how I got blown across Canada? Remember Australia? I am NOT going into a wind farm if I can help it!"

After a moment Eduardo spoke in a steady voice. "Stanley, I know how you feel. But as your friend, I have to tell you that you cannot run from your fears."

"What if I blow away?" said Stanley.

"We won't let anything happen to you, amigo," said Carlos.

"We won't even leave the car," said Arthur. "Promise."

Stanley swallowed and looked around at his friends. The only things that might be stronger than the wind, he thought, are friends like these.

"Okay. Let's go." He grabbed Arthur's hand and leaned back against the seat, taking deep breaths as Eduardo drove into the field of windmills.

Facing the Wind

Stanley watched the slender white base of one windmill after another zip past the car window. The truck was hot on their trail.

"Lose them, Eduardo!" said Carlos.

"Señora Lambchop said to drive safely," Eduardo replied. He kept his eyes fixed on the road.

"Maybe if we go in between the

windmills," said Arthur, "we'll be harder to follow."

Eduardo put on his blinker and carefully made a left turn off the main road. They slipped between two wind turbines. Eduardo made a right and then another left. White posts flew by in a blur. Soon Stanley had lost track of all the turns they'd made.

"I don't see them!" Carlos announced.

"We lost them!" agreed Arthur.

Stanley and the guys exchanged high fives.

But in the driver's seat, Eduardo had grown quiet. He was leaning over the steering wheel, looking carefully in one direction and then the other.

"What's wrong, Eduardo?" asked Stanley.

"I can't find the road we started on," Eduardo said. "And we're supposed to be at the Alamo soon."

"You mean we're lost?" said Carlos.

"We're going to be late?" croaked Arthur, checking his watch.

Eduardo said nothing. Stanley looked around. The windmills were identical and stretched in every direction.

"Try going back that way," Carlos suggested.

To turn around, Eduardo stepped on the brake and shifted into reverse. They lurched backward, and the car was jolted by a crunch. They had backed into a windmill. In a panic, Eduardo shifted the car into gear, and the car shot forward. *Crunch!* The front fender struck another windmill.

"Uh-oh," said Stanley under his breath.

Eduardo turned off the ignition. He spoke in a blank voice. "Señora Lambchop gave us only three rules. One: Drive safely."

"Too bad we just crashed," said Carlos.

"Two," continued Eduardo. "Meet her at the Alamo on time. And three—"

"Well, since we're lost," Arthur interrupted, "there ain't no way that's ever going to happen."

Stanley shot Arthur a look. "You mean 'isn't any way,'" Stanley said.

Arthur winced, realizing what he'd just done.

"And three," repeated Eduardo, "follow the rules of English grammar." He dropped his head to the steering wheel. "We have failed." He sighed.

Stanley couldn't bear to see his friends so upset. He suddenly realized how he could help . . . even if it meant doing what he was most scared to do.

"I know how to find our way out of here," Stanley said slowly. "Tie me to the rope and let the wind carry me up above the windmills. I'll be able to see the road."

Carlos shook his head. "Stanley, the wind—"

"I'll be okay," said Stanley.

"Are you sure, Stanley?" said Eduardo, raising his head.

"You guys have been there for me every step of the way," said Stanley. "It's my turn."

The boys all got out of the car to help Stanley get ready. His hands shook as he tested the rope around his body. There was a steady breeze in the air from all the windmills, and he had to struggle to keep his feet on the ground.

Stanley felt a bead of sweat roll down his face and all the way to his shoes. "I'm scared," he said simply.

Eduardo peered into his eyes. "Stanley, do you remember when you arrived in Mexico?" he said. "All the children thought you could not be hurt. We thought we could hit you like a piñata, and nothing would happen."

Stanley nodded.

"You told us we were wrong. Only then did we see how brave you were. Being brave does not mean you're not scared. It means you keep going even when you are."

"No one is braver than you, amigo," agreed Carlos.

"Except maybe me," teased Arthur.

Stanley nodded to his friends. Carlos and Arthur stepped forward, and together they helped lift Stanley into the air.

Releasing the rope a little bit at a time, Eduardo ensured that Stanley was carried up carefully between the windmills.

When the last bit of rope was let out,

Stanley floated above the wind farm, his body bobbing and flapping.

He surveyed the clear blue of the sky, the white sprouts of the windmills, and the brown of the earth. He called down to his friends. "The road is seven windmills that way!"

"Good work, amigo!" called Carlos.

"We're bringing you back down!" shouted Eduardo.

Stanley started to descend. Then there was a sudden jolt. The rope holding him had crossed a windmill's blades. The rope had been cut!

The wind tried to snatch him.

No! Stanley thought.

Without thinking, he rolled himself

up like he had after Eduardo's concert.
His stomach plunged as he dropped
from the sky like a stone. He could hear
his friends shouting.

He took a deep breath in and unrolled
himself at the last moment. The gusting

wind pushed him along the ground until he came to a rest . . . right in front of his friends.

The three boys stared down at Stanley in amazement and rushed to help him up.

"Are you okay?" Arthur said, gasping.

"I know what to do next time the wind tries to get me!" cried Stanley. "I just have to roll myself up!" He hugged his friends.

"Let's get out of here!" said Arthur. "Maybe we won't be so late after all!"

Showdown at the Alamo

As Eduardo followed the speed limit toward San Antonio and the Alamo, Stanley and his friends counted down the minutes until they were due to meet Mrs. Lambchop.

There was grim silence as the alarm on Arthur's watch went off: It was noon. They were late. Stanley hoped his mother wouldn't be too angry.

"Didn't something bad happen at the Alamo?" said Arthur. "Because I feel like we're about to be grounded forever."

Eduardo cleared his throat. "It was eighteen thirty-six. Texas had been ruled by France and then by Spain. Then it was a colony of Mexico. There was a terrible dictator, and the Texans decided to fight for their independence. More than one thousand five hundred

Mexican soldiers, against just a few hundred Texans, tried to take the Alamo. It was a long and terrible fight. The Texans lost—but they vowed to win after that. 'Remember the Alamo!' they said. Soon after, they beat the Mexican army and won their independence. That's why they call Texas the Lone Star State—because the spirit of independence here has always been so strong."

They arrived at last. The chapel of the Alamo had a roof that curved up in the center like a rising sun. The building looked like it had been standing for centuries and would stand for many more.

The boys climbed out of the car. In the distance, across the empty parking lot, Stanley's mother was waiting. Her feet were apart and her hands were on her hips. A dark frown hung on her face.

"Whatever happens," Arthur said, gulping, "we stick together."

Stanley and the other boys linked arms. The sun was high and sharp. A buzzard circled overhead.

Mrs. Lambchop took a slow step toward them. "I gave you three rules!" she called in a cold, stony voice.

The gang of boys stepped forward.

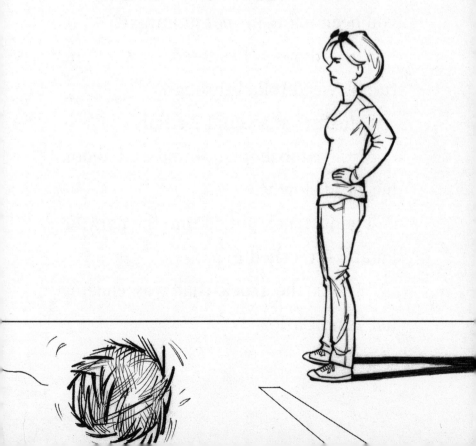

"And one of them was to show up on time," she continued and took another step forward.

"It was my fault!" Stanley, Arthur, Carlos, and Eduardo all said.

"I don't care whose fault it was," Mrs. Lambchop said. "A rule is a rule! Have you been using proper grammar?"

The boys hesitated. A lone tumbleweed rolled through.

"Mostly," answered Arthur.

Mrs. Lambchop squinted and shook her head slowly.

Then a truck pulled into the parking lot and screeched to a halt.

"That's the truck that was chasing us!" said Carlos.

The truck's doors swung open. In the glaring sun, Stanley could just make out the giant silhouette of a towering man in a cowboy hat. His boots ground the dusty asphalt.

Uh-oh, thought Stanley.

"We meet at last!" the giant cowboy said.

"They're mine!" called Mrs. Lamb-chop, moving closer to the boys.

Suddenly Stanley heard another voice as someone stepped from the passenger side of the truck. "Gol-durned fools!"

It was a girl. She tugged her leather vest and straightened her cowboy hat. She glared at Stanley and his friends.

Stanley's mouth fell open. "Calamity

Jasper! What are you doing here?"

"CHASING YOU!" she bellowed, charging toward them. "Ever since you sent me a postcard saying you'd be in Texas, I said, 'I just have to go visit my friends Stanley and Arthur.' I had my uncle Jeb drive me down here straight away!"

The giant cowboy tipped his hat.

"You know her?" Eduardo asked Stanley. "She was the one outside my dorm!"

Stanley slapped his forehead. "Calamity, I'm really sorry," he said, breaking away from his friends. "We thought you were one of my fans."

"One of your what?" cried Calamity Jasper. "Stanley Lambchop, when did your flat head get so big?"

"Probably around the same time he and his brother forgot to use proper English!" Mrs. Lambchop said.

"Well," Calamity said, "I'd wrangle them both to the ground myself, Mrs. Lambchop—except I'm so happy to see them!"

With that, Calamity pulled Arthur and Stanley into a hug. Mrs. Lambchop was right behind her. She hugged them too.

Then Mrs. Lambchop said, "I'm not happy you were late, but Stanley, wait until you see what the Texas librarians did! They made you into an activity! Students are sending cutouts of you through the mail!"

Just like that, the big showdown that Stanley had feared was over. And Stanley and his friends were still standing.

After they all toured the Alamo together, Uncle Jeb and Mrs. Lambchop went to the gift shop, while the five friends decided to play a game of Capture the Flag. Carlos and Calamity were on one team, and Eduardo and Arthur were on the other. The goal of the game was to capture Stanley, who was the flag, before the other team did. Stanley hung on to a flagpole, under a Texas state flag, just outside a window overlooking the Alamo courtyard.

It was Calamity who got to him first. She ducked under Eduardo's arm, grabbed Stanley, and jumped from the window.

She and Stanley sailed to the ground, with Stanley acting as a parachute. Arthur tackled them at once. Stanley

flew up in the air, curled into a ball, uncurled, and fluttered just out of their reach. His friends snatched at him madly, and soon all four of them were piled on top of him in the center of the courtyard.

They laughed and giggled, heaping themselves onto Stanley.

Nothing keeps me down to earth, thought Stanley, like my friends!

Flat Pal

A few weeks later Arthur and Stanley stood in a circle of friends in the schoolyard. Eduardo's song had become a big hit at school since they'd returned home and taught it to everyone. Now Arthur was pumping his hands through the air in the center of the circle and rapping:

"*Show your gratitude!*
Get the flattitude!

Rock like the kid

who rolls like a mat!"

Their friends made beats with their mouths and took turns singing verses. At the end of the song, Arthur pointed to Stanley, and Stanley leaped in the air, landed on his back, did some waves with his body on the ground, and flipped to his feet, his arms crossed. Everyone cheered.

It's not so bad having fans, thought Stanley.

Arthur and Stanley rapped all the way home, and people occasionally leaned out of their car windows to sing along with them. It was a blustery day, but Stanley kind of liked the way the wind brushed up against his feet.

Arriving home, the boys burst through their bedroom door.

Stanley was surprised to find two letters on his bed. One was from Eduardo, telling Stanley what he'd recently learned about the French Revolution. The other was from Calamity Jasper. Stanley opened the envelope and was surprised to see a small, flat figure fall out. But instead of being shaped like him, it wore cowboy boots, a worn brown vest, and a cowboy hat over its brown pigtails. Stanley flipped it over. On the back

it read "Next time, I'm travelin' with you, pardner!"

Stanley grinned and tacked Flat Jasper to his bulletin board, alongside all the other souvenirs from his adventures.

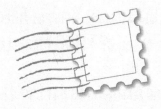

WHAT YOU NEED TO KNOW
TO GO ON YOUR OWN ADVENTURE
IN THE LONE STAR STATE

The city of Austin, Texas, is thought to be the live music capital of the world.

The capitol building in Austin opened on May 16, 1888. The building's dome is seven feet higher than the Capitol in Washington, DC.

"Álamo" is Spanish for cottonwood, which is a tree that grows in Texas.

The official state mammal of Texas is the armadillo.

There were only around 200 Texan soldiers who defended the Alamo against General Antonio López de Santa Anna's army of 1,800 Mexican troops!

The Battle of the Alamo was part of the larger Texas War of Independence. Texas became free after it won the war in April 1836.

"Remember the Alamo!" was the battle cry that Texans used after their defeat to recruit more volunteer soldiers for the next battle.

Even though Texas gained its independence in 1836, it didn't actually become part of the United States of America until 1845.

David "Davy" Crockett was a famous frontiersman and congressman from Tennessee. He fought in the Battle of the Alamo.

Texans turned the Alamo into a fortified fortress, complete with 21 cannons!

There's No Place on Earth
That a Flat Kid Can't Go!
Don't Miss:

Turn the Page to Read a Sample!

1

La Mission Impossible

Stanley Lambchop stood before the map that his teacher, Ms. Merrick, had yanked down at the front of the classroom. She nodded at him to begin.

"I've traveled all over the world," Stanley told his class. "I've been to Canada, Mexico, Egypt, Japan, Kenya, and China." He pointed to each country as he spoke.

His classmate Molly raised her hand. "Do you always travel by mail?" she asked.

Ever since the bulletin board over Stanley's bed had fallen and flattened him, he had been easy to fold and mail in an envelope.

"Not always. Sometimes I fly," Stanley replied. He thought for a moment. "On a plane, I mean. Or I can float thousands of miles if the wind is right."

Stanley's friend Carlos raised his hand next. "So you've never been to Europe?"

Stanley turned and found Europe on the map. He scanned the countries that made up the continent: England . . . Spain . . . France . . . Germany . . .

Italy . . . "Actually, no, I haven't been to *any* of the European countries. . . . But I *have* been to *Australia*." He reached over, past Europe and Asia, and proudly tapped the country in the bottom right corner.

The map shuddered and snapped up like a window shade. All at once it was dark, and Stanley's body felt very tightly wound.

He'd been rolled up with the map!

"Hilph!" Stanley cried. He could hear his classmates laughing.

Suddenly there was a muffled announcement over the loudspeaker. A moment later Stanley felt himself being unwound.

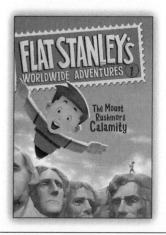